The Three Little Pigs

Retold by M. J. York

Illustrated by Laura Ferraro Close

BUILDING LITERACY AT HOME

You don't have to be a literacy expert to help your child become a strong reader. A few basic ideas and activities will set your child on the road to full literacy and prepare them for kindergarten:

READ TO YOUR CHILD DAILY. The most important thing you can do is set aside twenty minutes regularly—daily, if possible—to read aloud to your child. Your child's ability to follow and enjoy a story when read aloud far surpasses his or her ability to read independently. As you read, stop and talk about the story with your child. Ask questions and encourage your child to do the same.

TALK TO YOUR CHILD. Engage your child in lots of back-and-forth conversations. Ask them lots of questions. A home that's rich in spoken words helps a child's language development. The number of words heard at home from birth to age four accurately predicts how many words a child understands—and how fast they learn new words in kindergarten and beyond. And don't feel compelled to simplify your vocabulary. Complex conversations with sophisticated words are a good way to expose your child to rich language.

BE A READER, RAISE A READER. Simply having books in your home is enough to give kids an advantage. The presence of books sends an unmistakable signal to children about what their parents value. When a child sees a parent reading on his or her own, it reinforces the idea that reading is an important and valuable use of time. Take every opportunity not just to read with your child, but to demonstrate by example the importance of literacy in your own life.

We hope you enjoy reading The Three Little Pigs to your children this Christmas.
This book is a gift from The Mankato Area Foundation and The Child's World®.

Published by The Child's World®
1980 Lookout Drive · Mankato, MN 56003-1705 · 800-599-READ · www.childsworld.com

Acknowledgments
The Child's World®: Mary Berendes, Publishing Director
The Design Lab: Kathleen Petelinsek, Design · Red Line Editorial: Editorial direction

ISBN 9781614732167 · LCCN 2012932815
Printed in the United States of America · Mankato, MN · November, 2013 · GRP

O nce upon a time, an old mother pig and her happy family fell into misfortune. And so, she sent her three little pigs out into the world to make their own way.

The first little pig went out into the world. He soon settled down and built himself a little house of straw. Before long, a big, bad wolf came along and saw the little house of straw. He looked in the window and saw the first little pig inside.

The big, bad wolf knocked on the door and called, "Little pig, little pig, let me in!"

The first little pig cried, "Not by the hair of my chinny-chin-chin!"

"Then I'll huff, and I'll puff, and I'll blow your house in!" growled the big, bad wolf. And he huffed, and he puffed, and he blew the house down. The big, bad wolf found the first little pig and he gobbled him up!

The second little pig went out into the world. He soon settled down and built himself a little house of sticks. Before long, the big, bad wolf came along and saw the little house of sticks. He looked in the window and saw the second little pig inside.

The big, bad wolf knocked on the door and called, "Little pig, little pig, let me in!"

The second little pig cried, "Not by the hair of my chinny-chin-chin!"

"Then I'll huff, and I'll puff, and I'll blow your house in!" growled the big, bad wolf. And he huffed, and he puffed, and he blew the house down. He found the second little pig and he gobbled him up!

The third little pig went
out into the world. He soon
settled down and built himself
a little house of bricks. Before
long, the big, bad wolf came
along and saw the little house
of bricks. He looked in the
window and saw the third
little pig inside.

The big, bad wolf knocked
on the door and called, "Little
pig, little pig, let me in!"

The third little pig cried,
"Not by the hair of my
chinny-chin-chin!"

"Then I'll huff, and I'll
puff, and I'll blow your house
in!" growled the big, bad wolf.
And he huffed, and he puffed,
and he huffed and puffed
again, but he could not blow
down the house of bricks.

The big, bad wolf knew
he would have to be clever to
catch the third little pig. "Little
pig," he called. "I know where
to pick the sweetest turnips.
Come out and I'll show you."

"No, thank you," said the
pig politely. He knew the wolf
was trying to trick him. "I
don't like turnips." And the
big, bad wolf went away.

The next day, the big, bad wolf came back. "Little pig," he called. "I'm going to the fair. Will you come with me?"

"No, thank you," said the pig. "I have no money for the fair." And the big, bad wolf went away again.

The next day, the big, bad wolf came back once more. "Little pig," he called. "The best apples grow in Farmer Brown's garden. Come out and I'll show you where they are."

The pig knew the big, bad wolf would never leave him alone. He had a plan. "I'll meet you tomorrow at five o'clock," he replied.

The next day, the pig ran out of his house at four o'clock. He ran to Farmer Brown's garden. He picked a big basket of apples and ran home again. He put a big pot on the fire to heat water for his tea. The big, bad wolf came back at five o'clock.

"Little pig," he called. "Are you ready to go to Farmer Brown's garden?"

"I've already been and come home again," said the pig.

At this, the wolf grew angry. He had tried to trick the pig three times, and it had not worked. He wanted to eat the pig—NOW! He got a running start and leaped high into the air. He landed on the roof with a loud THUMP. He jumped down the chimney and—SPLASH—landed in the big pot of boiling hot water. That was the end of the wolf. And the little pig lived happily ever after in his little brick house.

BEYOND THE STORY

The Three Little Pigs is a popular fairy tale, told for many years to thousands upon thousands of children. You may recognize some of the lines, like "I'll huff and I'll puff, and I'll blow your house in," and "not by the hair of my chinny-chin-chin." These famous lines, as well as the big bad wolf and the three little pigs characters, have appeared in plays, musicals, books, and even movies like *Shrek*.

The Three Little Pigs story is not just a fun read. It teaches us a lesson, too. When you grow up and it is time to "make your own way in the world" like the three little pigs do, you can remember their story.

The first pig builds his house with straw.
Straw is very lightweight so it's easy to build
a house with, but the big bad wolf was able
to blow it away. The second pig uses sticks
to build his home. Sticks are easy to find and
lightweight, but also easy for the wolf to blow
over. The third little pig had to take more time
and effort to build his home from heavy bricks,
but it was solid enough to withstand the big
bad wolf's blows. And he is also smart enough
to think of a way to stop the wolf from coming
inside through the chimney.

Hard work and smart thinking pay off, as
we learn from the third little pig, the only one
still alive at the end of this tale!

ABOUT THE AUTHOR

M. J. York has an undergraduate degree in English and history, and a master's degree in library science. M. J. lives in a brick house like the Three Little Pigs and bakes bread like the Little Red Hen.

ABOUT THE ILLUSTRATOR

Laura Ferraro Close has been drawing ever since she can remember. She has also always had a love for piglets, so this story was fun for her to illustrate. Laura lives outside of Boston, Massachusetts with her husband, two teenage sons, and a sweet dog—but no piglets!